THE GIRL NEXT DOOR

AN EROTIC ADVENTURE

VICTORIA RUSH

VOLUME 6

JADE'S EROTIC ADVENTURES - BOOK 6

COPYRIGHT

The Girl Next Door © 2018 Victoria Rush

Cover Design © 2018 PhotoMaras

All Rights Reserved

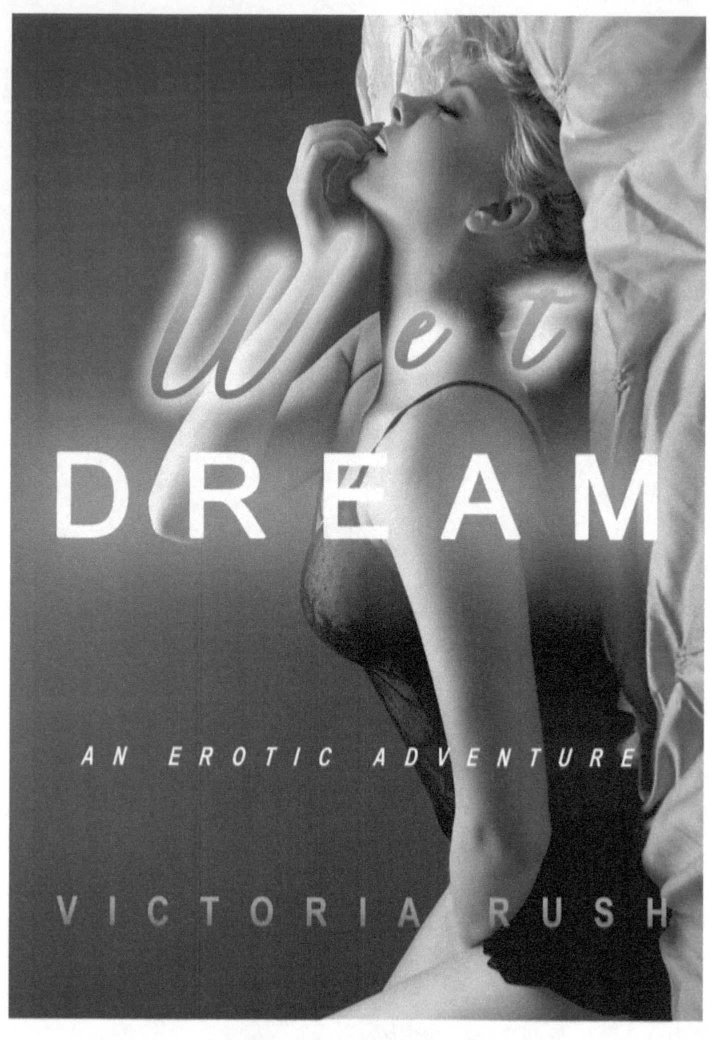

There's only one place you can live out your wildest fantasies...

Artificial intelligence never felt so real...

Everybody's an exhibitionist in disguise...

Books 6 - 10 in the bestselling series - now 60% off.

For the uninhibited...

1

KEEPING UP WITH THE JONESES

I 'd always considered myself a good neighbor. I'd kept my property in good repair, exchanged pleasantries whenever our paths crossed, and tried to respect everyone's personal space. But there's only so much privacy one can maintain when your homes are separated by a modest wooden fence. Especially when you live in a two-story house.

From my master bedroom balcony, I had a commanding view of my fellow residents' backyards. It didn't take long to figure out who lived in each abode, and everybody's predilections. Whether they liked to skinny-dip in their pool, sunbathe in the nude, or cavort in their hot tubs, it was pretty hard to hide from prying eyes.

Not that I made a point of spying on my neighbors. But the ones on my immediate west side were unusually reclusive. I knew they had a single teenage daughter because I'd seen her playing in the backyard when she was younger. But unlike all the other neighbor kids, she hardly ever left the house. She never got on the school bus rounding the neighborhood, and she rarely swam in their large in-ground swimming pool.

On the few occasions that she did venture into the water, it was always in a full-piece swimsuit. I watched her blossom over the years from a skinny pony-tailed girl to a full-figured, voluptuous young woman. With her shapely figure, long blonde hair and full sensuous lips, she looked like a young Marilyn Monroe. The perfect girl next door.

But I couldn't help feel sorry for how she'd been sheltered by her parents. There were no gentleman callers, no prom dates, no giddy sleepovers with her schoolmates. With her home-schooling, who knows what other worldly pleasures she'd been denied? The more often I caught fleeting glimpses of her, the more intrigued I became with her. I'd shamelessly spy through my shutters to catch a glimpse of her patting her wet body dry after a dip in the pool.

Counting the years since she'd fully developed, I figured she was approaching college age. One night, I knew a change was in the wind when I overheard her parents whispering on their back patio.

"We've got to let her go *one* day, Frank," a woman's voice said.

"I know, but college is such a huge step," a middle-aged man replied. "She hasn't been on her own her whole life."

"Abby's a smart girl," the woman said. "We've taught her well. She'll be fine. Besides, she's a grown woman now. If you ever want grandchildren, she'll eventually need to find a mate. Emory's a good Christian college. It won't be that big a leap for her."

"But it's halfway across the country—"

"There comes a time when every young person needs to spread her wings. This is Abby's moment to begin making her own way in the world."

"Miriam—"

"I've been thinking," the woman interrupted. "Summer's almost over. Why don't we take that trip to Europe we've been putting off for so long? We can have some time to ourselves and give Abby a little space to start looking after herself. That way it won't be such a shock when she leaves home."

"How long did you have in mind?"

"Two weeks. Enough time for us to do a little sightseeing and for Abby to get used to being alone."

"What if there's an emergency?"

"Aunt Jenny's only a half-hour away. Plus, Abby's got her driver's license and already knows how to cook and clean up after herself. How much trouble can an eighteen-year-old get into in two weeks on her own? We can call her every day if you're that worried."

The man sighed.

"All right, hon. I suppose we're going to have to let her be on her own one way or the other."

"Good. Because I've already booked the plane tickets for next week."

2

———

STOLEN GLANCES

In the days leading up to her parents' flight to Europe, all I could think about was Abby. She'd finally be alone, free to express herself and do anything she wanted. At the very least, I hoped she'd spend a little more time in her backyard. A late-summer heat wave had struck the city, and there'd be plenty of opportunities for her to take a refreshing dip in the pool. Maybe she'd been secretly harboring a two-piece swimsuit or — God forbid — planning a skinny-dip after dark. Either way, I'd be glued to my balcony in hopes of stealing another glance at her sweet, nubile body.

But after her parents left, I was disappointed to see her resume her sequestered ways. One day she left the house to pick up groceries and a couple of days later a middle-aged woman I presumed to be her aunt visited for a couple of hours. But during that first week, she ventured into her backyard only a few times to sunbathe in her one-piece suit. By the middle of the vacation fortnight, I began to despair of seeing any part of her beyond her bare legs.

One night as I was getting ready for bed, I noticed her

bedroom light was on later than usual. Our windows faced each other on the same side of our house, but she'd always kept her curtains drawn for privacy. Tonight though, I noticed a sliver of light emanating from a crack in the canopy. I crept up to the side of my window and separated my blinds with two fingers, then peered across the narrow laneway.

Abby was sitting at her desk, peering at a computer screen. She was wearing a light nightgown, and I could see the outline of her full breasts from the backlight of the computer through the gauzy material. The screen was flickering with some kind of moving image, but it was hard to make out what she was watching from my distance about twenty feet away. I reached into my nightstand and pulled out a pair of binoculars that I kept on hand for occasional neighbor spying.

Raising the field glasses to my eyes, I gasped when I adjusted the focus and zoomed in on her. The image on the screen was a porno, showing a man and a woman having missionary sex on a bed! I tilted my binoculars down a few inches and saw Abby had her legs spread apart with her hand moving in a strange thrusting motion between her thighs.

She's masturbating while watching the video!

I've never pulled my clothes off my body so quickly in my entire life. I stripped off my jeans and dropped my panties to the floor and immediately began circling my clit. My pussy was already soaked in excitement, as my juices ran down the inside of my legs. I struggled to steady the binoculars with my left hand as I furiously tribbed myself with my other hand.

As Abby watched the video, her mouth parted and I could see a pink flush on her cheeks. Her tits bounced up and down under her skimpy negligee as she rocked gently in her chair, while she thrust her fingers between her legs in rhythm with the lovers on the bed. I was just about to come when the man in the video lifted himself off his lover and stood by the side of the bed while she began to perform fellatio. Suddenly, Abby removed her hands from between her legs and lifted a strange green object in front of her face. It was a large cucumber!

Poor girl, I thought. *She doesn't even have a proper vibrator, having to resort to common household vegetables to get off.*

But what she did next soon made me forget about her deficiency of sex toys. She placed the end of cucumber in her mouth and began sucking on the tip, imitating what the woman was doing in the video. Then she moved her left hand back between her legs and began moving it rapidly up and down. I could see her body shaking in obvious pleasure as she sucked on the green phallus.

This girl is going to make at least one Christian college boy very happy.

The man in the video placed his hands at the side of the woman's head and began deep-throating her. I could see his butt cheeks contracting as he thrust his hips forward, while Abby mimicked his movements with her own rocking action on her chair. Suddenly the man stopped thrusting as he held the woman's head tightly against his stomach.

Abby pulled the cucumber out of her mouth and thrust it between her legs, then arched her back and moaned. I didn't realize that her window also was ajar a few inches, and the sound carried clearly over the small space between our houses. I'd hardly paid any attention to my own pleasure up to that moment, but when I saw her coming, I thrust my fingers into my snatch and gushed all over my hand, biting my lip to stifle my own screams of euphoria.

Abby rested for a minute with the cucumber still embedded in her pussy, then she grabbed the computer mouse and the screen flashed a few times before she settled on a new video. I turned my binoculars back to the monitor and noticed this time the video was of two naked women scissoring on the floor. Abby paused for a moment as I saw her eyes widen and her mouth part in surprise. Then she grabbed the cucumber with two hands and started pumping it into her cunny.

Fuck, that's hot! She likes women! Thank God.

My mind was already racing with thoughts of how I could entice her into my bed. But right now, I needed something in my *own* honeypot. I reached back down into my night table and pulled out my favorite vibrator, then I turned it on maximum and plunged it deep into my snatch. Abby and I were both fucking ourselves watching other women getting off, but suddenly Abby looked up and turned her head in my direction.

Had she noticed the movement in my window? I froze with the vibrator buzzing away in my pussy, suddenly aware that I was standing stark naked in front of my window with the shades half open. As she stared in my direction and squinted her eyebrows trying to detect any sign of intrusion, I suddenly came at the thought of her seeing me. My orgasm consumed me, and I struggled to remain motionless as my upper body quaked and quivered in powerful convulsions. I stared back at her, praying she hadn't noticed me.

When she returned her attention to her screen, I suddenly became aware of the dim glow that was being cast in my own room from my open bathroom door. I quickly walked over to the bathroom and turned off the light, then returned to the edge of the window and peered through the blinds. When I looked back up at Abby's window, she'd pulled her curtains and I could only see the faint shadow of her voluptuous body standing behind the sheers.

Fuck! I cursed.

Whether she'd been distracted by the flickering light in my room or she'd noticed me watching her, was unclear. Either way, I didn't care. I'd finally seen her magnificent body in all its glory, and we'd shared a powerful moment of pleasure together. And now that I knew she was sexually active and attracted to girls, I had other plans. I was already thinking of how I could escalate our secret rendezvous.

3

LAYING THE BAIT

I had difficulty sleeping that night thinking about what had happened between me and the girl next door. Beyond my obsessive thoughts of seeing Abby playing with herself, I couldn't help wondering why she'd left her window ajar. Had she just been trying to get some fresh air from the stifling heat of the day? Had she simply forgotten to close her curtains all the way? Or had she left them open *intentionally* hoping I'd see her?

Had she been watching *me* also all these years?

My mind raced with fantasies of fucking this shy vixen. Even though she was all grown up, she'd probably never felt the delicate touch of another man or woman. Her mother was right—Abby needed to find her own way in the world, and soon. College would be crawling with thousands of predatory men trying to take advantage of such a beautiful innocent girl. She needed to be educated in the ways of tender lovemaking before getting a rude awakening.

After watching Abby fuck herself with the huge cucumber, I rushed downstairs to retrieve one from my own fridge. I was startled at first by the feel the cold vegetable in my pussy, but it didn't take long to warm up inside my steaming love tunnel. There was something about the texture and feel of the cucumber that made it feel almost like a real cock. Unlike my vibrator, it had a certain sponginess to it. It had the firmness of a man's hardon, but it was flexible like the real thing. The lack of artificial vibration, far from being a detriment, actually was a welcome change from my oscillating dildo. It felt like a real man inside me—just a better hung one. Maybe Abby wasn't so deprived after all. As I lay on my bed with splayed legs replaying the image of Abby pumping her pussy with the giant legume, I got an idea.

I watched for any sign of movement from Abby the next day, but her curtains remained closed and she didn't venture outside. I still harbored hope that the little glimpse she'd provided me the previous night wasn't just a coincidence. At dusk, I repositioned my bed against the opposite wall so that it was directly facing my window. Then I opened my blinds half way and slid the window open a few inches. I turned on my night table lamp so that it cast a soft glow over the covers. Then I took off all my clothes and lay face up on top of my sheets and closed my eyes.

If Abby happened to glance out her window, she'd see me stark naked, looking like I'd fallen asleep trying to catch a break from the heat. But I had a lot more than just *sleeping* on my mind tonight. I squinted through half-closed eyelids at Abby's window for over an hour but didn't see any sign of movement. It was approaching 10:30 p.m., and I assumed she'd soon be getting ready for bed. Eventually, I saw some flickering light coming from behind her curtains.

No, Abby! Look out your window, not at your computer! I'll give you a much better show than any of those pornos, and it'll be the real thing.

I squeezed my thighs together in frustration, then

remembered what had brought her to her window yesterday. I leaned over and turned my night table lamp on and off twice in rapid succession, then I leaned back down. Through the corner of my eye, I could see her shadow moving behind the thin curtains. Then I noticed the corner of the drape open on one side and a dark figure blocking the light from her room. She was looking out her window! I knew she could see me clearly across the laneway in the soft illumination of my bedroom in the pitch dark of night. Now it was just a question of whether I could maintain her interest.

I shifted my position as if I was having a restless dream while keeping one eyelid open just enough to see her outline through the window. She didn't move. But I had to be careful. I didn't want to make it look like I was luring her into some kind of a trap or make her feel uncomfortable. I still wasn't sure that she'd seen me yesterday or that she knew I'd seen her. I needed to maintain the illusion that I was sleeping, or at least that I hadn't noticed her watching me from across the laneway.

I lifted my right hand off the bed and let it flop on my stomach like I was unconscious. Then I began to shift my hips in rhythmic movements as if I was having an erotic dream. It was electrifying to know that Abby was watching my naked body just as I had watched her the previous night. After a few minutes of suggestive hip action, I felt daring enough to begin fondling my tits. I cupped my left breast and began pinching my nipple while continuing to sway my hips. Abby was locked in position by the edge of her window. I knew I had her. Now it was just a matter of pulling her in.

After a few more minutes of squeezing my breasts and writhing suggestively on the sheets, I began to move my left hand down my stomach towards my pussy. I paused for a moment with my fingers on the edge of my pelvic bone while I lifted and swayed my hips. My bare pussy throbbed in anticipation of my touch. The thought of Abby watching me perform my tantalizing tease was intoxicating, and I felt the wetness accumulating on my lips.

I glanced out the corner of my eye and detected some movement of the curtain near the bottom of Abby's window. Her hips were swaying in synchronicity with mine behind the curtain. She was getting just as turned on as I was! I spread my legs further apart and moved my left hand slowly down over my pubis. Trying to play with yourself while pretending to be asleep was more difficult than I thought, and I wasn't sure how much longer Abby would buy the ruse.

But it no longer mattered. As long as I had a captive audience, I intended to make the most of it. I'd give her a show she'd never forget while enjoying something I'd never experienced before. I'd taken this whole spying-on-the-neighbors thing to a whole new level. When I finally touched my clit, I flinched in pleasure. My button was already poking out from under its hood and it was flaming hot. I mixed in the juices from my sopping pussy and circled my nub as I lifted and swayed my hips for my private audience.

I could have come right away, but I wanted to savor the moment and make it last. Plus I had a lot more in mind for the education of my innocent voyeur. I could feel the juices running down my vulva onto my ass, and I moved my other hand between my legs and began to fuck myself with my fingers. My pussy began to make sexy slurping sounds and I moaned loudly as I felt the pleasure rising in my belly.

Suddenly, I heard the sound of Abby's window sliding

open as she shifted her weight a few inches away from the edge of her window. She'd obviously heard my muted moans through the glass and wanted a clearer connection. The drapes parted a little further, and I could see the full outline of her hourglass hips against the backlight of her bedroom. Before the curtains closed again to a narrow sliver, I caught a glimpse of a dark patch between her legs.

Of course she'd be unshaven, I thought. *She probably doesn't even know what all the girls are doing these days in terms of intimate grooming.*

Her natural appearance made me even more turned on, and I fucked myself harder as I imagined kissing her furry mound. My orgasm was getting closer, and I began thrashing my hips on my bed while I circled my clit with one hand and fucked myself hard with the other. Abby's curtains parted a little further, and I saw her hand moving between her legs under her thin negligee. That was enough to put me over the edge, and I screamed like a wild animal as I came. I no longer cared if Abby thought I was asleep or not, I just wanted to let the pleasure pour out of me. I heard a little peep emanate from Abby's window and I saw her knees buckle as her chest jerked in rhythmic spasms behind the curtain.

My contractions lasted for almost a full minute as I clamped my hand inside my pussy, giving Abby a full view of my naked body in the throes of ecstasy. After I finally calmed down and stopped moving, I noticed Abby was still standing at the side of her window with the curtains slightly parted.

That's my girl, I thought. *Stay there, baby. Momma's got a lot more where that came from.*

I flipped over, stretching my arms and legs lazily, and lifted my bare ass in her direction.

If you like the front of my body, wait till you see my backside.

I was proud of how I'd maintained my body tone for my age. Regular workouts at the gym and the yoga studio had kept my ass firm and round and tight. I spread my legs slightly to give Abby a glimpse of the dark tunnel between my legs, then I began to raise and lower my ass, beckoning her in. It felt sexy showing her my backside, but from my prone position, I could no longer see what she was doing in her window.

I reached over to my nightstand and tilted my phone up against the front of my clock radio, then twisted it until I could see Abby's reflection on the screen. The dark glass provided a perfect view of the illuminated window across the dark passageway. I wasn't sure if she could see my reflection as well, but it must have been obvious what I was doing, and she didn't flinch away.

Now that I'd reestablished our two-way line of communication, I returned my attention to my aching pussy. I slid my hands under my hips and spread my legs further apart, then placed my fingers under my mound and began fingering myself with both hands. I was still at the height of arousal from my last orgasm and knew it wouldn't be long before I came again. As I began to hump my bed, contracting my buttocks in rhythm with my hands, I heard some moans emanating from Abby's window.

At this point, I had no more interest in carrying on the illusion that I was half asleep. I lifted myself up on all fours and spread my ass cheeks to show Abby my soaking snatch. She had a commanding view of my open pussy and ass, and I leaned my shoulders down on the bed so she could also see my tits hanging between my legs. I reached around with my left hand and plunged my fingers into my cunt while I jilled my clit furiously with my other hand.

I was grunting like a wild animal at the thought of Abby watching me fuck myself from behind. But there was still one thing missing. I reached under my pillow for the cucumber that was still coated with my slippery juices and slammed it into my ass.

I bet this is something you haven't yet seen in one of your pornos!

I looked in the reflection of my phone and noticed that Abby was no longer standing at the edge of her window, hiding behind the curtains. She had pulled them aside and was standing in full view of the open window, with the back-light from her room shining through her flimsy negligee. I could see her full breasts bouncing on her chest as she rubbed her pussy frantically.

She was moaning without abandon now, and I joined her in our shared pleasure. My orgasm hit me without warning, and I couldn't help screaming her name as I gushed onto my hands and clamped down on the cucumber embedded in my ass. Abby screamed out loud too, and the whole neighborhood must have heard our cries of ecstasy as we climaxed in glorious union.

I knew now, that this was going to be the start of a glorious friendship.

4

———

HEAT WAVE

When I woke up the next morning, Abby's curtains had been pulled back and I could clearly see into her room. A small four-poster bed was neatly made up with pink throw cushions and linens. A tall bureau sat next to it with a collection of stuffed animals resting on top. In the far corner, a large pink dollhouse sat unused on the floor. Overhead, a fan with Alice-in-Wonderland leaf-shaped blades whirled quietly on the ceiling. Other than her computer desk and bookcase filled with high school home-study books, it looked like a typical young girl's bedroom frozen in time.

But for most of the morning, there was no sign of Abby. I wasn't sure what to make of the conflicting signals. She'd finally opened a portal to her world, which couldn't have been a coincidence. But why was she being so coy staying hidden? Was she feeling embarrassed about the intimate moment we'd shared the previous night? Had she noticed me watching her in the reflection of my phone on the night-stand? Why would she open her drapes if she didn't want me to see her?

Just before noon, I heard the front door of her house open and close, and I rushed to my living room to peek out the window. She climbed into a Toyota Echo sitting in the driveway, then backed up and turned in the direction of downtown. Was she going to visit her Aunt? Was she heading out to replenish her groceries?

Or was she going to the police station to complain about her peeping Tom neighbor?

For the next couple of hours, I paced my house second-guessing whether I'd pushed the envelope too far. I still wasn't entirely sure she was even of legal age. What if she'd taken a *video* of me? Could that be used to prove that I was some kind of criminal, trying to lure an under-age child into illicit sex? My mind raced with all manner of scary scenarios, with patrol cars screeching into my driveway and burly policemen hauling me off to jail.

After a couple of hours, my heart rate finally returned to normal when I realized the cops would have already arrived at my door if she'd intended to report me. But I knew I had to be far more discreet in my outreach efforts going forward. There could be no more private nude shows, at least until I verified she was eighteen. I used the free time waiting for her to come back to formulate a plan.

I figured it couldn't be easy for her cooking her own meals for the first time in her life. It must be overwhelming having to cook and clean and look after that big house all by herself. I resolved to bring her a ready-made dinner that night. If she was amenable, I'd invite her over to my place, where I could take care of all the details and free her from having to worry about cleaning up. But what kind of food did she like? What does a sheltered home-schooled teenager like for dinner?

After some deliberation, I decided to bake her a chicken

casserole. Chicken was pretty safe, and if she didn't accept my invitation, it would be easy for her to simply heat it up in her oven. I could toss a fresh salad as a side, and offer her a glass of wine to help her relax. But not until I verified her age. I probably wasn't the only nosy neighbor checking out the comings and goings in the neighborhood. The last thing I needed was to get either one of us in trouble for underage drinking. Or underage sex.

Jeesh. How could I broach that subject delicately?

I decided to run out to stock up on fresh groceries, and when I returned I noticed Abby's car in her driveway. I hurried inside and rushed upstairs to my bedroom. When I peered out my window, I saw that Abby had closed her drapes again.

Now what? I thought. *Is she having second thoughts about what she'd seen last night? Had she only opened the window to let in a little fresh air from the oppressive heat?*

I walked onto my balcony and peered into Abby's backyard. It was quiet as a mouse. If she planned to retire back into her shell, I had one last chance. There was no harm in being neighborly by offering to share a meal I'd baked. At least this way, I could confront her directly and see if she was as interested as I was in her. For the next hour, I focused on preparing the casserole, while keeping my eyes and ears open for any sign of activity from next door.

Just as I was placing the baking dish in the oven, I heard the distinctive sound of someone diving into a pool. It sounded like it came from Abby's side, and I raced upstairs to peer out my balcony into her yard. When I glanced at the pool, I saw Abby's unmistakable form swimming across her pool.

But this time, she was wearing a skimpy yellow two-piece swimsuit. I watched her tight round bottom wiggling through the water as the yellow shorts clung to the crack in her ass. As she turned her body from side to side, the side of her firm breasts rose tantalizingly above the edge of the water before plunging again below the surface. I was absolutely mesmerized watching her magnificent figure slide through the churning water.

After four or five laps, she stopped at the end of the pool closest to me and lifted her head out of the water, then shook the drops from her hair. She glanced up in my direction and I quickly slunk back behind my bedroom door. I was sure she'd seen me staring at her again, and I cursed myself for being such a pussy. This cat and mouse game, as sexy as it was, was getting tiring.

I went into my bedroom and pulled a racy romance novel out of my nightstand then turned the chair on my balcony towards Abby's house and sat down. If she caught me peering in her direction, I didn't care. I was simply catching some sunshine on a warm day while enjoying a good book. If she chose to run around in a skimpy bikini, that was her business.

When I returned to the balcony, Abby was standing by the side of the pool toweling herself dry. She seemed to linger longer than usual patting her breasts and the area between her legs, and I could have sworn I saw her glance up in my direction again. I tried to hold my gaze on my book, but I wasn't reading a single word. I peered over the top of the paperback, trying to cover as much of my face as I could get away with.

Abby walked over to the side of her pool near her back fence where two chaise lounge chairs rested, and she reclined one of them to a flat position. Then she placed her towel on the cushions and lay down with her backside pointed directly in my direction.

You little tease, I thought.

The ball was now in Abby's court. She was being just as sneaky and calculating as I'd been. Now it was *her* turn to put on a show for me. At first, she simply lay quietly on the lounge, pretending to soak up the sun. But after a few minutes, she began to shimmy her hips in the same manner I had the previous night. I smiled as I parted my legs, my pussy flooding with juices. I suddenly wished that I'd placed some kind of barrier between me and the narrow railing spindles of my balcony to provide more privacy. But I dared not move for fear of missing a single twitch of Abby's exquisite body.

After a few minutes of rolling her hips seductively, she shifted her arms from over her head and rested them at her sides beside her ass. Then she lifted her hips and moved her right hand under her pelvis.

Holy Fuck! I gasped out loud. *She was going to finger herself in plain view, just as I had yesterday!*

There was no longer any doubt that she'd seen me watching her the previous nights. She was going to torment me in exactly the same way I'd done with her. I glanced around at my fellow neighbors' properties to check that we were alone. It was a hot weekday afternoon, and most people had either retreated inside their air-conditioned homes or were lying around their fenced-in pools. Abby had chosen her lounging position carefully, close to the back fence where no one else could see her besides me. Had she also purchased that skimpy yellow bikini today to drive me even more crazy?

I raised my right leg and bent my knee to provide a modicum of cover, then I unzipped the front of my shorts and thrust my fingers under my panties. As I watched Abby's fingers moving in the tight cleft between her legs, I circled my clit and groaned in delirious pleasure. My shorts already had a giant wet spot creeping down the front of my pant legs, as I dripped like a broken faucet watching her play with herself.

I could see Abby's buttock muscles flexing as she humped the chaise lounge cushion. She was faced away from me, so it was hard to see the expression on her face, but I remembered the sweet look of ecstasy I'd seen two nights ago. I looked in front of her to see if there was any reflective object where she might watch me like I had with her last night, but there was none. Apparently, she was content to give me a one-way show.

But then she turned her head to the side and flitted her eyes in my direction. I could tell that she was trying to disguise the fact that she was peeking at me out the corner of her eyes, and I laughed when I realized how obvious it had been when I tried a similar feint last night. I lowered my book and spread my legs as far as I dared as I rubbed my soaking snatch furiously. We both stared at each other for a moment, then her lips parted and I could hear soft moans wafting up to my balcony. This time I couldn't wait for her. I jerked in my chair and pulled my legs together as I came all over my wet hand in my shorts. I groaned out loud from the pleasure sweeping over me, as I shook and convulsed in my chair.

She must have seen me in the throes of orgasm, because within seconds, she suddenly straightened her legs and pointed her toes, and she clenched her cheeks together as her upper body began to shake. We didn't take our eyes off each other the whole time we both came. The feeling of our first direct visual connection was electrifying, and I spasmed in my chair for almost a full minute as I watched the pretty girl in yellow release her inhibitions for the whole world to see.

Two hours later, I knocked on the front door of Abby's house carrying my ready-made casserole. It took quite a while for her to come to the door, and I began to worry that I'd scared her away. If I were in her shoes, I'd be a little nervous too about making direct contact with someone I'd shared such an intimate, but heretofore remote, relationship.

Maybe her parents told her not to open the door for strangers, I thought. *Come on, Abby. You can do this. I won't bite.*

About sixty seconds later, I heard some footsteps approaching the door from the other side, then I saw the view hole flicker as she looked through the spyglass. She hesitated for a moment, then swung the door open.

"Hi," I said. "I'm Jade, your next-door neighbor."

Abby's pupils dilated as big as saucers. Whether it was from excitement or nervousness, I couldn't be sure.

"Yes," she said. "I recognize you. I've seen you...*around*."

"I hope you don't mind this little intrusion. But I saw your parents leave for a trip a few days ago and noticed that you were all alone. I thought I'd be a good neighbor and bring you a little gift."

I held the covered baking dish in my outstretched arms.

"That's very thoughtful," Abby said. "What is it?"

"It's a little casserole I threw together. It's already cooked. You just need to put it in the oven for thirty minutes to warm it up."

Abby reached out and accepted the dish, then we paused awkwardly for a moment on the doorstep.

"If you'd like, we could share it together," I said. "If you want to come over to my place, I could throw together a nice side salad and we could get to know each other a little better. We've been neighbors for quite a while, and I heard rumors that you'll be heading off to college soon. I'd love to hear about your plans."

Abby hesitated as her eyes fluttered considering the offer. She must have known I had other designs, beyond sharing a meal together.

"Um, okay," she finally said. "When's a good time?"

"How about seven?" I said, trying not to betray the rush of excitement coursing through my body.

"Okay, I'll see you then."

Abby smiled at me, then she closed the door. I practically skipped back to my place with thoughts of what lay ahead that evening.

5

THE SWEETEST WINE

For the next two hours, I busied myself preparing for Abby's visit. Fortunately, I'd replenished my fridge earlier in the day and had most of the cooking already done. Now it was just a matter of cleaning up the house and getting myself ready. I washed the sheets and placed some extra cushions on the bed, then cleaned the washroom and hung some fresh towels. I wasn't sure if Abby would make it this far, but I wanted to make everything as welcoming as possible if she did.

Then I had a long shower, dried my hair, and put on some skinny jeans and a silk blouse. I knew I was over-dressed for a casual dinner, especially on such a hot day, but I wanted to highlight my best assets in hope of attracting Abby's attention. I considered going braless, but at the last minute erred on the side of prudence over provocation. I didn't want to be too obvious or make Abby feel like I was coming on too strong.

When my doorbell rang at seven that evening, I rushed to the door and took a deep breath before swinging it open. Abby looked more beautiful than ever in matching pastel shorts and blouse, with tasteful leather sandals. Her shimmering blond hair was freshly washed, and she'd applied some light lipstick and mascara that highlighted her natural beauty. My eyes lit up as she stood on the doorstep holding a beautiful bouquet of long-stemmed tulips.

"Abby," I said. "Come in. You look...*lovely*...this evening."

Abby stepped over the threshold and presented the flowers to me.

"Thank you, they're gorgeous. How did you know tulips were my favorite?"

"I didn't, but they're my favorite too. I thought I should bring something..."

I took the flowers from Abby's hands and motioned toward the other end of the house.

"Come to the kitchen while I place them in a vase. Are you hungry?"

"Yes, definitely," Abby said, smiling at me softly. "It's been a while since I've had a good home-cooked meal."

I led Abby into my kitchen and filled a tall vase with water.

"Where did your folks go for vacation?" I asked.

"France, mostly. They were going to spend a week in Paris, then a few days on the Mediterranean coast before taking the train to England and flying back from London."

"How lovely. I hear the French Riviera is beautiful at this time of year. May I ask why you didn't join them? It would have been a perfect going-away gift."

Abby shook her head and shrugged her shoulders.

"They didn't ask. Maybe they just wanted a little alone time. I've been a bit of a handful all these years, with the home schooling and everything. This is the first time any of us have had a real break from one another. Maybe they wanted to make sure I could look after myself before sending me off to college."

I nodded my head as I sprinkled some flower food into the vase.

"College is a big step, especially for someone who hasn't had any prior public education. Are you excited?"

"I have to admit I'm a little scared *and* excited."

Abby watched me for a moment as I clipped the flower stems and arranged them in the vase.

"Do you mind my asking how you knew my parents were going away?" she asked.

I stopped for a moment and looked up.

"Yes, I guess that was a little forward of me. I actually overheard them talking one night on your patio by the pool. Voices carry pretty easily up to my balcony on a quiet night."

"Is that how you knew my name too?"

I placed the vase in the middle of my dining room table then looked up at Abby.

"Yes, sorry if I've been such a nosy neighbor. But it was nice to put some names behind the familiar faces. We've lived next door to one another for so long and never been formally introduced."

Abby frowned as she shifted position uncomfortably.

"My parents are a little overprotective of me. I think it was their religious upbringing. Not wanting me to have any unholy influences, and all that."

"Well there's a lot of *sinful* activity out there," I said, smiling at Abby. I placed a head of lettuce on the cutting board in the middle of my kitchen island and began chopping it into little pieces. "Is that why you so rarely ventured out of the house also?"

"You mean into our backyard, using the pool?" Abby said.

"Among other things."

"After I started developing, they didn't want me exposing my body. When they bought the house, it came with the pool. But they thought I'd be desecrating myself if I exposed too much of my body to strangers."

I shook my head as I sprinkled the lettuce leaves into a salad bowl.

"It's a shame, because you have such a lovely figure. I don't see any harm in displaying your God-given features, if you do it in a tasteful way. I was glad to see you sharing a bit more of yourself by the pool yesterday."

Abby looked away from me and blushed.

"Did you like the new swimsuit?"

"Oh, yes," I said, pulling a large cucumber out of the fridge and plopping it on the cutting board. "I enjoyed it very much. You looked absolutely ravishing in it."

Abby blushed a deeper shade of crimson and turned her body to look through my kitchen window into my backyard.

"You have a lovely home. I see you have a pool also. Do you use it very often?"

Watching Abby stand by the window made me think she'd stolen just as many glances of me swimming half-naked in my pool as I had of her.

"As often as I can. Especially in this summer weather. It's a great way to cool off from the heat." I grabbed a large paring knife and began slicing the cucumber into thin slices. "I especially enjoy swimming in the nude after dark. The water feels magnificent on my naked skin."

Abby shifted uncomfortably as she glanced toward her own backyard.

"That sounds like fun, but my parents would kill me if they ever caught me doing that."

My pussy began to moisten at the thought of watching Abby's naked body snaking through the water.

"You've still got a few days before they return. You should try it. It's very invigorating."

"What about the neighbors? There's not much...*privacy*...with us all huddled so close together."

I smiled at Abby's double entendre. I was beginning to enjoy our little game of verbal brinkmanship.

"If you do it quietly with the lights off, no one will notice. Except maybe the ones who've been watching you ever since you've grown up."

Abby turned around when she heard me pull the casserole out of the oven.

"The dinner smells delicious. Thanks for having me over."

"It's been a pleasure getting to know you, Abby," I said. "Please, have a seat." I uncorked a bottle of wine and paused as I held the open bottle over her goblet. "Are you old enough to drink?"

"I just turned eighteen last month."

"Well we'd better start getting you acclimated," I said, breathing a huge sigh of relief. "God knows, there's going to be plenty of spirits flowing once you get to college."

For the next hour or so, Abby and I made small talk over dinner, talking about her course of study and plans after college. Neither of us broached the subject of what we'd seen and done over the last couple of days, but by her second glass of wine Abby had loosened up and begun to talk about dating. When I started clearing the table and placing the dishes in the sink, she offered to help clean up.

"How about if I do the washing and you help me dry?" I said, handing her a dish towel.

As I filled the sink and leaned over to pour some soap in the water, I caught Abby stealing a glance at my ass.

"So you like boys, then?" I asked.

"I suppose so, but my parents haven't let me go on any dates yet. I'm not sure I'm ready though."

"Really?" I said, passing her the wet casserole dish. "You're eighteen, in the prime of your life, and just about to head off to a place that will be teeming with eligible bachelors. What's your hesitation?"

"I don't know," she said, rubbing the inside of the baking dish gently with her towel. "Lately, I've been finding myself more attracted to...*women*. I'm beginning to wonder if I'm—"

I turned around to face Abby and gently took the casserole dish from her hands and placed it on the counter.

"Abby, you're a smart, beautiful, sexy young woman. Anyone will be lucky to share your love. You'll know when the moment comes what the right decision is..."

I leaned toward Abby's face and hesitated as we peered into each other's eyes. Abby closed the distance and placed her lips softly against mine. Our hips moved together, and I placed my arms around her back and pulled her closer. My mind began spinning as we both moaned in each other's mouths.

I wanted to fuck her right then and there, and it was tempting not to lift her up onto my kitchen counter and pull off her shorts. But I glanced through my kitchen window and realized that we were far too exposed to prying eyes.

"Let's go somewhere where we have more privacy," I said.

I took her by the hand and led her upstairs to my bedroom, then gently lay her down on top of my comforter. I kneeled down beside her and propped myself over her body as I drew my right thigh up between her legs and pressed it against her warm pussy. Abby took in a sudden breath of air, and we gazed into each other's eyes as I lowered my face onto hers. As we kissed passionately, I pressed my mound into the soft flesh between her legs. Abby moaned into my mouth, and her breathing became ragged.

After a few minutes, I lifted myself up and began unbuttoning her shorts, but Abby placed her hand over mine to stop me. I feared that she might be having second thoughts, but then she leaned forward and glanced out my bedroom window.

"Do you mind if I close your blinds?" she said. "I know my parents are away, but it'll make me feel more secure. You never know who else might be watching from a distance."

I smiled and nodded knowingly.

"Of course," I said. "This time, there'll be no one but the two of us."

Abby got up off the bed and walked to the window, then turned the shutter handle to close the blinds tightly. When she walked back toward me, I stood up and blocked her before she reached the bed. Then I looked into her eyes and began unbuttoning her blouse. She looked straight back at me as I separated her blouse and peered at her breasts. She was wearing an old-school brassiere that pulled her breasts tightly together, and I stared at the cleft produced by her large bosom. I reached around her back with two hands and unclasped the latch of the bra, then I raised it and gasped.

Abby had the most beautiful breasts I'd ever seen on the female form. Full and plump, they were perfectly round and firm, sitting high on her chest. If I didn't know better, I might have thought they were surgically enhanced, but of course she was far too young and sheltered to have gotten anywhere near a plastic surgeon. Her areolas were small and dark, with thick nipples protruding almost a full inch off her chest. I cupped her tits with both hands then buried my face shamelessly between her magnificent mountains.

When I lifted my head, I sucked gently on each of her erect nipples. Abby placed her hands behind my head and moaned softly as I licked and stimulated her sensitive teats. I wanted to feast on her like a suckling baby, but the throbbing clit in my wet pants reminded me there was much more to enjoy. After a few minutes of kneading, suckling, and playing with her melons, I finally pulled myself away and kissed her on her lips.

"You're exquisite," I said, looking into her eyes.

"Jade," Abby panted. "Take me. I've been waiting for this for so long."

I pulled Abby's blouse off behind her back, then lifted her bra over her shoulders and threw it softly on the edge of the bed. Then I unbuttoned the front of her shorts and pulled them over her round hips and let them fall to the floor. I was surprised to see her wearing plain white granny-panties that extended almost up to her belly-button.

Jesus, I thought. *I'm going to have to take this girl to the mall to get her properly outfitted for college. This is no way to present herself among trendy university students.*

I placed my fingers under her waistband and slowly pulled her panties down over her stomach. When the band got half way down her abdomen, a tuft of light brown hair puffed out, forming a perfect triangle in the cleft between her legs.

She really hasn't been touched down here at all, I thought.

My mouth watered at the thought of feeling her downy pubic hair against my face.

Abby's legs quivered as I pulled her panties over his hips and lowered them to the floor. I kneeled down in front of her and untied her sandals, as I rolled my head softly against her bush. I could hear Abby panting above me, and I smiled in the knowledge that she was enjoying being touched by another woman for the first time.

When I finished untying her sandals, I placed my arms around her thighs and kissed her on her mound. I breathed in the fresh sweet scent of her pubic hair and closed my eyes. There was something about her natural beauty that was driving me absolutely crazy. As I kissed and nuzzled her soft muff, I raised my hands and cupped her ass.

"God," I muttered audibly, when I felt her firm round cheeks.

Her ass was even more perfect than her tits, if that were even possible. I desperately needed to see her full body in all its naked glory. I stood up and took a step back to look at Abby. She stood with her hands beside her hips, her tummy shaking in anticipation and excitement.

"You're stunning, Abby," I said, taking a long pause to soak up every curve and valley of her magnificent figure. "You're even more beautiful than I imagined."

Abby stepped forward and began clumsily unclasping the buttons on my silk blouse, then I took a step back and motioned for her to stop. I slowly unfastened the buttons myself, taking my time to sexily remove every stitch of my clothes while her eyes grew wider and wider and her stomach fluttered in obvious excitement. When we were both finally naked, we took a moment to appraise other's bodies, then we pressed our bodies together and began kissing passionately.

Abby was a clumsy kisser, unsure what to do with her tongue, and I slowed her down to teach her the proper technique. I placed my hands gently on the sides of her cheeks and began by softly kissing the sides of her lips. I nibbled her lower lip for a few seconds, coating it with my saliva, before inserting my tongue gently into her mouth and swirling it softly inside her. Then I placed my hands beside her head and pulled her into me, turning my face and head to probe her sweet, pliant mouth. As we rubbed our tits and pussies together, Abby's breathing grew heavier and heavier.

I desperately wanted to thrust my fingers into her box and feel her wetness in my hand and give her her first real live orgasm. But I kept reminding myself this was her first time with another lover and that she deserved a tender and measured first experience. After five minutes of passionate kissing, I separated myself again and grabbed Abby's hand and led her to the bed.

I lowered her softly onto the covers, then lay beside her on the bed. We turned and pressed our breasts together and kissed gently for the longest time. I just wanted to feel her delicate skin against mine and breathe in her sweet aroma. My mind spun in a drunken stupor, I was so elated to be finally holding her in my arms.

But there was so much more I wanted to do with her, and before long we separated again and I slowly began kissing my way down the front of her belly. I could feel Abby's stomach shaking the closer I got to her honeypot, but when I reached her mound, I stopped and kissed her soft muff for several seconds. It had been so long since I'd seen or touched a full and natural pubic patch, I reveled in the softness of her downy fur.

Abby twisted and raised her hips, begging me to go lower, and I gently spread her legs apart. I could smell the sweet aroma from her cunny and knew that she wanted me to touch her there. But I began by kissing the insides of her thigh, tantalizingly edging my way up toward her steaming kitty. I wanted to take me time and give Abby the most amazing sexual experience of her life.

When I finally reached her apex, her thighs were already coated in her juices. I placed two fingers over her opening and ran them along the sides of her slippery labia. Abby had a beautiful pussy, with full and plump outer lips framing tight, symmetrical inner lips. Everything about her was like she'd been molded by God himself to create the perfect female form.

Abby whimpered as I played with the outer edges of her flower, then I slowly inserted two fingers into her hole. She grasped my fingers tightly as I pressed them into her, then I began to slowly finger-fuck her as I watched her head roll from side to side in delirious pleasure. I couldn't believe that I actually had my hand inside this gorgeous angel, giving her a pleasure she'd never yet experienced. How lucky was I to be the first one to touch her virgin garden?

Abby began rolling and thrusting her hips more vigorously, and I began to fear she might come before I had a chance to taste her nectar. I lowered my head between her legs and placed my mouth over her throbbing clit, then I sucked her nub between my lips. Abby gasped and raised her hips off the bed, pushing her pussy harder into my face. It felt glorious to finally feel her in my mouth, and I danced my tongue over her clit as I listened to her squealing in unbridled pleasure.

"Yes!" she moaned. "Suck me, Jade. Please suck me. I want to come in your mouth."

I almost came myself when I heard her mention my name, and I clamped my thighs together, trying to give my aching clit some direct stimulation. I could feel Abby's clit hardening in my mouth as her hips thrashed and pressed against my face. I knew she was close when her whimpers turned to squeals, and I curled my fingers toward me, stimulating her G-spot. Suddenly, she lifted her hips off the bed and grasped the side of my head with two hands and squeezed my ears tightly.

"Jade!" she screamed. "I'm coming! God, I'm coming!"

With one final guttural groan, she paused and held my head between her legs as she jerked and spasmed against my drenched face. I could feel the inside of her pussy clamping down on my fingers in rhythmic contractions, as I cradled her softly, savoring every pulse and squirt of her quivering body.

6

———

TWO BECOME ONE

Abby and I lay quietly on my covers after she came, kissing and caressing each other, as her breathing slowly returned to normal. I ran my hand over her torso, marveling at the size and firmness of her breasts. Even lying down, they pointed high and proud on her chest, like the twin pyramids of Giza. I cupped and squeezed and pinched them, like a child with playdough.

"Are you sure you these things aren't surgically enhanced?" I said, pinching my eyebrows in amazement.

"Are you kidding? My parents would never let me debase what God gave me."

"Well thank you, God, for bestowing this beauty with such perfect and natural gifts. You're really a work of art."

I traced my hand further down her belly and ran my fingers through her soft pubic patch.

"I love your muff, too. It's so soft and...*pure.*"

Abby looked between my legs then placed her hand gently on my mound.

"Really? I noticed most of the girls in the videos are

shaved like you. You're so smooth—there's no stubble like when I shave my underarms."

I smiled at Abby's delightful innocence.

"I used to have it waxed off, but a few months ago I chose to have all my pubic hair removed with laser treatment. Let's hope the trend with intimate landscaping doesn't change anytime soon, because there's no going back for me."

Abby caressed my mound softly with her hand, then pushed her fingers lower between my legs.

"I like it," she said. "I can feel *all* of you."

I watched Abby's eyes widen as she ran her hands over my bare vulva.

"You know I spied on you a couple of nights ago watching those videos. It was super-hot. Did you leave your drapes and window open on purpose?"

Abby lowered her gaze shyly as she caressed my inner thighs softly.

"Yes. I was kind of hoping you'd notice me. I've been spying on you for years. Watching you get dressed in the morning, sleeping at night..."

I placed my hand under Abby's chin and lifted her face so I could peer in her eyes.

"Is that what you were doing *last* night too?"

"Yes," she sighed. "You were so beautiful and sexy, I couldn't take my eyes off you."

"Did you like the little show I put on for you?"

"Yes. You were very naughty."

"Apparently, we both have a certain affinity for long green vegetables."

Abby blushed, then pressed her tits against me. Her hand circled over the back of my ass as her fingers probed between my legs.

"What can I do for *you* now?" she said. "I want to give you the same kind of pleasure you just gave me."

"Well actually," I said, lifting myself up off the bed. "I had a little something in mind that I think we might *both* enjoy."

I slithered down toward the other end of the bed and positioned myself between Abby's legs.

"No fair!" Abby said, trying to raise herself up. "It's *your* turn. Shouldn't I be the one on top this time?"

I pressed Abby back down onto the bed and smiled.

"There's a lot of ways to have sex besides the missionary position, young lady. Remember that video you were watching the other night? How would you like to try that?"

Abby began to roll and lift her hips seductively.

"Mmm—yes, please. I want to feel you. I want to feel you...*fucking* me."

I raised my eyebrows, then a wide grin stretched across my face.

"You're so naughty. I *like* a naughty girl."

"Show me how you do it, Mommy," Abby said, continuing the role play. "Show this innocent church girl the ways of the world."

"Fuck, yes," I growled.

I pulled her hips toward me and scissored my legs under and around her midsection. When our pussies touched, we were both sopping wet, and I could feel the heat radiating from Abby's oven. She moaned loudly when our clits connected.

"Oh, Abby, I've dreamed of doing this to you for so long. Let Momma cum all over your sweet cunny."

I got up on my knees and pushed my steaming pussy against Abby's hairy snatch and began grinding our hips together.

"Fuck," Abby panted. "That feels so good. Fuck my cunt with your beautiful bald pussy!"

I couldn't believe Abby was talking dirty to me, which turned me on even more. I lifted her right leg off the bed and placed it between my tits as I humped my pussy between her legs. I could feel her wetness coating both of our thighs and our pussies made sexy squishing sounds as our labia rubbed together. Abby's tits shook like two huge Jello molds as she looked between her legs watching me fuck her.

"God, yes!" she panted. "Fuck me, Jade. I want to watch you come like you did for me. I love you."

When Abby said those words, I felt a surge of energy through my body and my pussy tingled in excitement. I pushed my mound hard against hers and wrapped my arms around her extended leg on my chest.

"Abby!" I said, looking straight into her eyes. "I'm going to come baby. I'm going to come all over your sweet virgin cunny."

My climax poured over me like a tidal wave. I pulled Abby's leg hard against my chest and squirted my love juices into her gaping hole.

"Fuck," I screamed. "I'm cumming, Abby! I feel you between my legs. Come with me!"

Abby suddenly opened her mouth like she was gagging, as a deep red flush swept over her chest above her tits.

"Yes," she screamed. "Feel me, Jade! I'm cumming with you. Ohhh, yesssss!"

Abby grabbed my hips and pulled me toward her as we thrashed and ground our pussies together, screaming and panting in ecstatic union. I could feel Abby's fingers digging into the sides of my buttocks as her hips jerked and spasmed in concert with mine. All the while, we never took our eyes off one another. When we finally stopped coming, I held Abby's leg tightly against my chest for another minute as I savored the feeling of our wetness comingling between our joined pussies. Then I collapsed onto the bed beside her and exhaled deeply.

"That was incredible!" Abby panted. "I feel blessed that you're my first."

I turned my body toward Abby and kissed her gently on her lips.

"I'm the lucky one. You're an angel sent down from above. I've never felt—"

I stopped myself before I said something I'd regret. Abby was just starting out in her voyage of exploration, and she was just about to head off for college. It was unfair of me to harbor any expectations beyond our little fling.

"You mean..." Abby said. "You feel it too? Do you—"

I placed my finger over Abby's lips, then I pushed myself back so I could look at her directly.

"You've got your whole life ahead of you, Abby. I'm almost old enough to be your mother. You deserve to experience all the wonders of youth and explore your sensuality with other young people. Some day, long after you've graduated and found your footing in the world, you'll find your soulmate. We'll always have a special connection, and I'll always be your friend, forever."

Two streams poured down Abby's cheeks as her face contorted in pain.

"Does this mean we can't be...*lovers* any longer?"

I pulled Abby toward me and hugged her close to my body.

"We'll always have this special bond, Abby. But I want you to be free to fall in love with other people, to find that special someone you'll be perfectly yoked with. Right now, I think it's mostly the hormones talking."

"What do you mean?"

"Well, when two people make love and have an orgasm together, there's some special hormones that are released that causes them to have certain feelings for one another. It's called the love hormone—oxytocin. Nature, or God, provided us with this so that we'd be more likely to stay together and raise the children that often come after coupling, to ensure a more successful family unit."

"But...we're women. We can't have children this way."

"It's the same hormone, no matter who you're with. And it's a very powerful hormone, like a drug. You'll find it has a similar effect with other people you're attracted to. Don't rush into love—let it find you."

Abby snuggled closer to me and kissed my neck.

"Well whatever those hormones do, I like it. If we can't be lovers, can we at least be *friends with benefits* a little longer?"

I pushed Abby away from me and opened my eyes in mock surprise.

"So that's it? You're going to dump me just like that? Wham, bam, thank you ma'am?"

Abby looked at me coyly and traced a circle around my nipples with her fingers.

"Not exactly. I was hoping we could do a little more whamming and bamming, at least before I go off to college. I'm guessing there's a few more things you can still teach me..."

I flipped Abby over onto her back and pulled myself on top of her.

"You're damn right there is. In fact, I did have something else in mind if you're not too tired and already spent."

"Are you kidding? I'm eighteen! I can come all night with you if you'll let me."

"All right then," I said, getting up off the bed. "You just wait here and keep that pretty little pussy of yours warmed up for me. I've got a little surprise for you."

I hurried downstairs and ran into the kitchen and flung open the fridge. Then I opened the crisper and looked at the special collection of cucumbers I'd purchased at the grocery store earlier today. I picked out the longest and thickest one and bent it gently between my two hands.

This one will do just fine, I thought.

I ran back upstairs holding it behind my back and skipped into my bedroom like a kid on Christmas, stopping a few feet from the bed with a huge Cheshire grin on my face.

"What?" Abby said, a big smile spreading on her face. "What are you hiding behind your back?"

I slowly pulled my arm around in front of me and held the giant cucumber up triumphantly in front of me.

Abby looked at me teasingly and shook her head.

"But we've both already tried that. I thought you were going to teach me something new!"

"Oh, but there's so many ways we can use a big dildo like this," I said, crawling onto the bed between Abby's legs. Let Mommy show you how else one can savor fresh cucumber."

I placed the sprout against the inside of Abby's thigh, and she flinched from the cold texture on her warm skin. Then I slowly slid it up the inside of her thigh until it pressed against her pussy. She gasped when it touched her, and I began to slide it up and down over her wet slit.

"That feels good," Abby purred.

"It feels even better when it's *inside*," I said. "But you already knew that. This is what I mean about experimenting with other people. You really won't know for sure if you just like women until you've felt a man's throbbing cock inside you."

Abby looked up at me, surprised.

"So you don't just like girls?" she said.

"I consider myself *pansexual*," I said. "I like to have sex with the right person in the moment. But I have to admit, I do have a special fondness for women..."

I thrust the tip of the cucumber into Abby's hole and she took a sudden intake of breath.

"Yeah?" I teased. "You like that? There's more where that came from."

As I pushed the cucumber further inside her, I watched it stretch and push her labia apart the further it went.

"Uhnnn," Abby groaned. "Yes, Jade. Fuck me. Fuck me with your big cock."

I began to pump the cucumber in and out of her as I watched her head roll from side to side in pleasure. She thrust her hips in a matching humping action as she fucked and squeezed it in her tight box.

Damn, I thought. *This girl is going to make one hung dude very happy some day. But right now—she's all mine.*

"Deeper," Abby panted. "Fuck me deeper with your big cock, Jade."

I already had about seven or eight inches buried inside her and could feel the end of it pushing up against some resistance.

"It won't go any deeper," I said. "I don't want to hurt you."

Abby tilted her head up and peered at me holding the other end of the vegetable.

"You've only got it half way inside me," she said, teasingly. "It seems a shame to waste so much of it."

I smiled at Abby knowing we had the same idea.

"You're reading my mind, girl. I had no intention of wasting the other half."

I lay down on the bed and spread my legs facing Abby, then I slithered my pussy towards hers and inserted the other end of the cucumber into my slit. As I pushed myself toward her, I could feel the cucumber pushing deeper inside me. Abby groaned as she felt the pressure of it pushing inside her from my movement.

"God, yes!" she panted. "Fuck me, Jade. Fuck me with your big green cock."

I continued twisting and pushing the cucumber inside me until it filled me up. When our pussies finally touched, Abby and I both moaned, then we began rocking our hips together as we fucked the big dildo from opposite ends.

"Ohhh, Uhnnn," Abby groaned, as I clamped down on the dildo and thrust it inside her pussy.

We alternated squeezing and releasing the cucumber within each of our pussies, exchanging the feeling of being fucked and fucking our partner. This was something I'd never experienced before, and I closed my eyes focusing on the incredible sound and feel of the giant cock sliding in and out of our pussies as we ground our clits against one another. Within a few minutes, I felt that familiar sensation rising within me and knew I couldn't hold out much longer.

"Baby," I called out to Jade. "I'm going to come again. Let me feel you gush all over my cunt as we come together. Are you ready?"

"Yes," Abby panted. "I'm going to come all over you. Fuck me hard!"

I sat up and placed my hands beside Abby's hips, pulling her toward me in rhythmic movements as I thrust the cucumber deeper inside her. It was an incredible sight watching the thick green phallus going in and out of her splayed pussy as I fucked her like a man. As I felt my orgasm take hold of me, I squeezed Abby's buttocks and pulled her crotch hard against mine.

"Come for me, baby," I cried. "I'm going to come inside you now. Feel me, Abby," I yelled. "I'm *cumming!*

Abby and I both screamed each other's names as we gushed all over the slick cucumber embedded deep within our pussies. I could feel the walls of my pussy contracting as it gripped the fleshy dildo, and my clit twitched against the hard, cool skin of the vegetable. It was the most incredible feeling coming together with Abby, joined as we were with the juicy object between us.

We shook and panted and whimpered for several seconds, as we climaxed together. When we both came down from our highs, I pulled the wand out of our pussies and lay down beside Abby at the head of the bed. I placed the slippery cucumber between our tits and slid it sexily between our breasts, then I sucked on the end that had been in Abby's pussy.

"Mmmm," I said, looking teasingly into her eyes. I much prefer my cucumbers this way than in a salad."

For the rest of the week, Abby and I played and made love with each other, trying our best to stay out of the public eye. I was mindful that her parents would be returning from vacation soon, and I didn't want any nosy neighbors spilling our little secret. We pulled the blinds shut then slept together, ate together, giggled together, and bathed together. And we fucked each other deliriously, right up until the last moment.

After her parents returned, we continued our remote

affair through our adjoining windows at night, with nobody the wiser. On the day Abby left for college, she snuck over to my place and gave me one last, long lingering kiss. Then I didn't hear from her again until she returned home for the Christmas holidays. Although I missed our secret trysts, I smiled whenever I thought of her, knowing that she'd finally found her independence.

Also by Victoria Rush:

CLICK FOR MORE INFORMATION

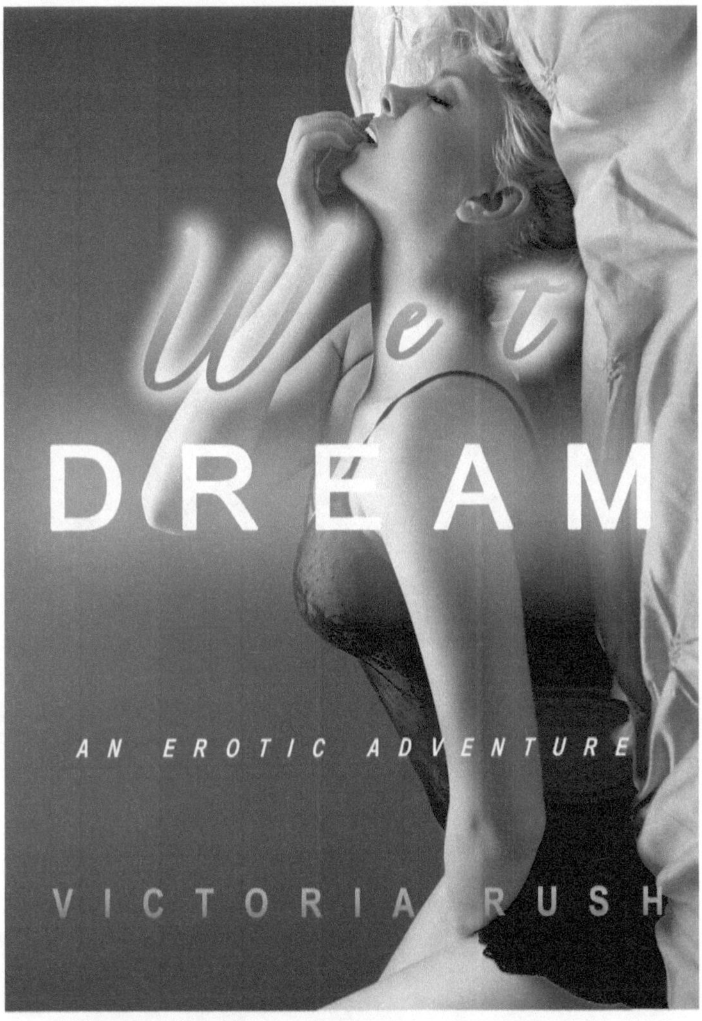

There's only one place you can live out your wildest fantasies...

Artificial intelligence never felt so real...

Everybody's an exhibitionist in disguise...

Books 6 - 10 in the bestselling series - now 60% off.

GIRLS' CAMP - PREVIEW

After we finished eating, Lilly placed the entrails and fish heads back in the water, then we washed our cutlery and bagged up our plates and hung our trash from a rope over a high tree branch to keep the bears away. As dusk set in, we built our fire back up and huddled around the pit in a circle.

"What now?" Hannah said. "What do six girls do for fun after dark on a lonely island in the middle of nowhere? Tell spooky stories?"

"*Stories* could be fun," Maddie said. "But they don't have to be spooky. I'm already creeped out enough about the idea of sleeping in that flimsy tent with so many bears within swimming distance. How about some *fun* stories?"

"I know!" Bonnie said. "Let play *Truth or Dare*. That outta get our juices going. Who wants to go first?"

"Truth, or *dare*?" Hannah asked.

"Truth," Bonnie said. "Tell us something daring about yourself that none of us know."

"Hmmm," Hannah said, looking up trying to think of

some sordid detail from her past that she was willing to share. "Well—I once spent a night in jail."

"No way!" Emma said, her eyes widening in disbelief.

"*Way*," Hannah said. "Though granted it was only for a couple of hours. I was sixteen and got caught for shoplifting. I think the sheriff in my small town wanted to make an example of me to scare the shit out of me."

"Did it work?" Lilly asked.

"I wasn't really scared, because I was all alone in my cell and I kind of knew what they were trying to do. I was more scared about what my father was going to do to me when he bailed me out."

"And?" I said.

"Grounded for three months. Which is like three *years* when you're sixteen. So yeah, I guess it worked insofar as discouraging me from doing something like that again."

"What did you steal?" Bonnie asked.

"A vibrator from the local sex shop. I was too embarrassed to actually buy it, so I tried to sneak it out under my coat instead."

"That'll teach you to play with naughty things before your time," Lilly winked at Hannah.

"What about *you*, Lil?" Hannah said. "What naughty things have you done that we don't know about?"

"*Welll*," Lilly said, stretching out the word for dramatic effect. "I engaged in some technically illegal sex not too long ago...."

"Mmmm, *yummy*," Hannah said. "Do tell. There's not many things that are illegal anymore in that area."

"It was an underage boy. *Sixteen* to be exact. The captain of my son's football team. We were at the boy's parents' house celebrating their championship and he and I were alone having a chat, and one thing led to another. We slipped into the ravine behind his yard and had a quickie."

"A *quickie*?" Hannah teased. "That hardly sounds like fun. Was he nicely hung at least?"

"He definitely came equipped with a decent package. But you know boys at that age. They can't last very long—"

"What exactly did you two do?" I probed for more details.

"I just gave him a quick blowjob. I was too terrified we'd be found out. But it was fun and definitely satisfying."

"For at least *one* of you!" Madison said.

"I suppose," Lilly said. "How about you, Maddie? What kinky things have you gotten into that we don't know about?"

Maddie paused for a moment trying to conjure up a sufficiently juicy story.

"Well, my husband and I just had anal sex for the first time last week—"

"Which *one*?" Hannah said. "You or *him*?"

"*Hannah*!" Bonnie scolded, shooting Hannah a disapproving look. "That's prying a little too deep. Let Maddie tell the story."

"What?" Hannah said. "I'm just saying, she could have used a strap-on, or something. Some guys are into that sort of thing—"

"It was *me*, if you must know," Maddie said. "I mean *receiving*, that is."

"What's that like?" Emma said, scrunching up her nose in disgust. "I mean, doesn't it hurt?"

"Oooh," Hannah teased. "I guess we know at least *one* of us has never tried this. Poor little Emma, leading such a sheltered life..."

Emma lowered her head and frowned as she peered into the fire. I wanted to walk over to her log and put my arms around her. It was cruel of Hannah to put her on the spot like that and make her feel small.

"Well it didn't hurt exactly," Maddie continued. "But I wouldn't say I enjoyed it as much as the usual way. My husband certainly did though, judging by his moans of delight."

Everybody paused for a moment as the girls looked at me and Emma to see who would go next. Hannah glanced over at Emma still sulking on her log and finally broke the silence.

"What about you, Jade? What kind of fun adventures have you been up to lately? I mean besides sleeping in and working on your graphic design projects?"

I looked at Hannah with a sly smile. If she *only* knew. I probably had accumulated enough kinky stories just in the last couple of months to outdo everybody around the campfire. But I still wasn't ready to share my most personal secret.

"Well, I recently had a little remote affair with one of my neighbors..." I started.

"*Remote*?" Hannah said. "As in not face-to-face? Was it telephone sex or webcam sex?"

"Neither. We just watched each other through our windows at night. It was actually pretty hot."

"Oh? Is this someone you've had your eye on for a while? Is he hot? What did you guys do?"

"Yes, I've had my eye on him for a while now," I lied, not wanting to tell the girls that it was actually Abby, the college girl next door. "We've been watching each other around our adjoining pools for some time. But he's married, so I never felt comfortable making the first move."

"So, what did he do? Flash you from his private study while his wife was doing the dishes?"

"I think his wife was away for a few days. It was late at night, and I caught him coming out of the shower with his bedroom light on. I guess he caught me watching him and one thing led to another..."

"So you both rubbed one out watching each other?"

"Yeah. But it was just a one-time thing. His wife came home the next day and I didn't want to take any more chances at getting caught."

"Well that definitely qualifies as semi-hot," Lilly said.

Everybody turned to Emma, who glanced nervously out of the corner of her eyes at the rest of the group.

"That just leaves you, Em," Lilly said. "What sordid details have you been holding back about yourself?"

Emma paused for a long moment as she glanced at her friends around the campfire.

"Well, I once did it with a...*girl*. You know, at college."

My panties instantly moistened as I squirmed uncomfortably on my log.

"It was with my roommate. We were both pretty drunk after a party, so I'm not even sure it qualifies—"

"Oh, I think it *definitely* qualifies," Hannah said. "You've got to give us at least a few details. What did you two do exactly?"

"You know, the usual stuff. There's only so many things two girls can do together, right?"

"*Boo!*" Hannah jeered. "Not good enough. You've got to give us at least one detail."

"Well," Emma hesitated. "It started with us both lamenting how neither of us had hooked up in a long time. One thing led to another, and we ended up making out on my bed."

The more I listened to Emma, the more I could feel a large wet spot spreading in my cargo pants between my legs. I shimmied toward a knot on my log and quietly rubbed my clit against the stump in the dark as Emma told her story.

"*Making out*?" Hannah said. "What do you mean? Kissed, fondled, sucked, scissored—we want details!"

I could see Emma shifting nervously on her log, beginning to feel uncomfortable about sharing any more details.

"You know," I interrupted. This whole time we've been telling truths and we haven't even had a single dare. I've got a dare for everybody. I dare you all to strip off your clothes and go skinny dipping in the lake with the big old muskies and snapping turtles!"

"If we don't get eaten alive by the *mosquitoes* first!" Bonnie protested.

"Not if we get in the water fast enough," I said, stripping off my clothes. "Last one in a rotten egg!" I scampered over the pine needles of our campsite and ran into the water at our little beach.

"Come on in, you scaredy-cats!" I taunted from the water. "The water's warmer than the air. It's like taking a bath."

The rest of the girls quickly disrobed and scurried into the water, where we splashed and spit water at each other's faces and playfully dove under the surface groping each other. After about ten minutes, we all scampered out of the water and toweled dry, then rushed into our tents and zipped up the flaps to keep the mosquitoes out.

I scolded Hannah for putting Emma on the spot earlier, then we talked a little bit about work before falling asleep early from all the sun and fresh air. But about thirty minutes later, I woke to the sound of rustling not far from our tent. Thinking it might be a bear foraging through our camp, I was about to wake Hannah when I heard the unmistakable sound of a woman moaning. I lay perfectly still and held my breath straining to listen.

The sound was coming from the direction of Bonnie and Emma's tent. I lifted the privacy flap up over the mosquito net window on my side of the tent and peered into the darkness. They'd left a small flashlight on inside their tent, and I could see the shadows of two figures lying next to one another, rubbing their bodies together.

They're making out! I thought.

Suddenly, I wished I'd tried harder to pair up with Emma in her tent. I was envious of Bonnie having her all to herself. Obviously, Emma's story had gotten more than just *me* worked up, and after they'd returned to their tent stark naked, one thing had led to another.

Fuck! I whispered out loud, thrusting my hand under my sleeping bag, beginning to circle my clit.

As I strained to catch whatever I could pick up from the tent next door, I began to hear gasps and moans radiating into the still night. I couldn't make out if it was Emma's or Bonnie's voice, or both of them. But it didn't matter. I was insanely turned on just listening to them, trying to imagine what the two of them were doing.

I squinted through the mosquito netting trying to discern their movement, but I just saw a jumbled clump of shadows shifting in the soft backlight. Suddenly, one of the figures rolled on top of the other, and I saw the unmistakable shape of a naked ass raising and lowering onto the person beneath.

Oh my God. Now they're humping each other!

I wanted to dash out of my tent and join the girls in their fun and feel Emma's sweet pussy between my own legs. *Oh—how much pleasure I could give her,* I thought. I sped up the movement of my fingers over my clit, trying to control my breathing and movement so as not to wake Hannah.

Suddenly, the figure on top raised up to a kneeling position and the girl on the bottom pulled her legs up into a bent knee position. Then the girl on top squatted over her and lowered herself onto her partner below. When the girl on top began shimmying her hips, I saw her full breasts swaying in the backlight and realized for the first time that Emma was on the bottom.

Emma doesn't have tits that full and round, I thought. *Bonnie's full-on fucking her!*

I could hear the women's breathing becoming louder and more ragged, building toward a climax. I jammed two fingers into my cunt and began thrusting as hard as I dared without waking Hannah from the squeaking of my air mattress shifting on the soft ground below us.

Suddenly, the moans escalated in urgency, as Emma thrashed her head from side to side in the throes of pleasure.

"Yes, Bonnie!" I heard her whisper. "Fuck me harder. I'm going to come!"

My pussy suddenly clamped down on my fingers as my orgasm washed over me, and I bit my lip trying to stifle my moans.

"I'm coming, Bonnie!" Emma whispered. "Come with me! Fuuuck—I'm coming!"

Bonnie sped up the humping motion of her hips against Emma, then she suddenly stopped as I saw her chest and torso jerking spastically in the soft backlight.

"Uhnnn," she grunted, as she came inside Emma's sweet tight pussy. "Fuck, yes," she said. "I'm coming, baby!"

I twitched and spasmed inside my sleeping bag as I came along with the two girls, trying desperately not to awaken Hannah sleeping mere inches beside me. When Bonnie finally collapsed on top of Emma and their light switched off, I rubbed out two more orgasms before falling blissfully asleep with the warm stickiness between my legs.

Read More...

ABOUT THE AUTHOR

If you would like to receive notification of new book(s) in Jade's Erotic Adventures, follow me at http://bookbub.com/authors/victoria-rush.

If you have a moment, please post a brief review on my Amazon book page at viewbook.at/tgnd . Even just a couple of sentences will help other readers find and enjoy this book as much as you hopefully did.

Follow, share, like, and comment at:

www.facebook.com/authorvictoriarush
www.pinterest.com/authorvictoriarush
www.twitter.com/authorvictoriarush
authorvictoriarush@outlook.com

Hope to see you again soon!